To Chloe, who hates cabbages.

© 1991 Diz Wallis
Lettering by Paul Stickland
First published in 1991
by Ragged Bears Limited, Ragged Appleshaw,
Andover, Hampshire SP11 9HX
All rights reserved
Printed in Hong Kong
ISBN 1 870817 58 3

SOMETHING NASTY in the CABBAGES

by Diz Wallis

A tale from ROMAN DE RENARD
written in the 12th century by
Pierre de Saint-Cloud
and retold for this edition by
the artist

Ragged Bears

There was once, not so very
long ago, a farm which was
owned by Constant and his
wife. Here they are, looking
cross. Next to the farmyard
was a cabbage patch, where
the hens lived and here
they would strut and scratch
and peck, fat and content,
amongst the cabbages. They
were quite safe from all
intruders because Constant
had built a solid fence with
high oak stakes and sharp
hawthorn. This made a
barrier so tight and prickly
that even the leanest,
hungriest fox could not
squeeze through.

There never were such
happy hens...

Now here is someone who knew the hens well and his name is Reynard. The sight of the plump hens made his mouth water for he was always famished, yet he knew he could not catch them because of the spiky barrier that stood in his way. So he would run round and round it, jumping up and lying down, craning his neck to see if there might be some way he could break in.

Imagine, then, his pleasure, when one day he found a broken stake. He couldn't believe his luck. He scrambled over and dropped quietly down into the cabbages on the other side.

At this moment proud Chantecler, the cockerel, was dozing on the dungheap in the corner of the cabbage patch. One eye was closed and one eye was open for he had to keep guard over the hens. He felt this was his duty, even when he was asleep.

Suddenly there was a flurry
of feathers and much
squawking and chattering
and all the hens rushed
towards Chantecler.
"Whatever is the matter?"
he crowed at them.
"We saw the fence shake,"
they squawked, "we saw the
cabbage leaves tremble,
some horrid, hungry beast
is hiding amongst the
cabbages, waiting to eat us
all."
"Pooh! Monsters amongst
cabbages, whatever next?
You silly birds, nothing
could get in here without
my seeing it. Go back and
feed," And he dismissed
them all with a shake of his
glossy feathers.

But something had got in...

The sunlight on the steaming heap sent him back to sleep again. This time he had a dreadful dream. Something nasty was out there in the cabbages. It crept up softly, slowly, dragging behind it a red fur coat with a bone collar. It flung this pelt round poor old Chantecler tying him up so tightly in it, he thought he might die. As soon as he awoke, though his legs shuddered and his crest shook, he hurried over to where the hens were hiding and told them all about it.

"Oh! Layers of enormous eggs! Tell me what it
means," he begged.
"This coat," they said, "is a fox's coat, and the collar
of bone, it's teeth. Teeth that will seize and swallow
you, unless you run and hide. He's out there now.
Hide Chantecler." But Chantecler was already feeling
braver. "Huh! Hide? What me?... No fear. I can take
care of myself!" he crowed.

Oh proud and foolish bird!

Puffed up with pride at his own importance he made his way back to his noble perch, and before long he began to nod off again quite unaware of what was creeping up, crawling up underneath the cabbages! Barely a leaf twitched, scarcely a twig cracked, for a fox is the king of stealth. His eyes glinted in the shadows, and when Chantecler seemed fast asleep, he pounced. But the cockerel spotted him at the last moment and sprang out of the way and up the mound. He crowed as loudly as he could with relief. "Cock-a-doodle-doo!"

The fox was vexed but he didn't show it. He stood at the foot of the dungheap as if spellbound. "What a magnificent voice you have! It's almost as good as your father's, but he used to close his eyes to sing. It helped him to reach those higher notes. Won't you try it?" Chantecler was suspicious, but he wanted to prove he could outsing anyone. So he closed one eye and crowed, keeping the other firmly fixed upon the fox. "Almost," said Reynard in a charming voice, "but to reach the very highest note you must close both. Come a little closer and sing to me again." So Chantecler, flattered and convinced, did as he was told, closed both his eyes and sang!

Reynard, seizing the chance, fell upon the bird and carried him off leaving but a feather or two to flutter down upon the mound.

"Didn't we tell you so?" wailed the hens in the distance. "How you mocked us and scoffed at us and wouldn't listen. Now see where your pride has got you." But fox and cockerel were already over the fence and out of earshot.

Just then the farmer's wife
came to the gate to call her
hens in for the night. They
didn't come and she felt
uneasy. Then she saw what
had happened – the fox had
made off with her cockerel.
She called for Constant,
who ran to her side.
"That wretch Reynard has
made off with my
Chantecler!" she screeched
at him.
"Well why didn't you stop
him?" he yelled.
"Stop him? Do you think he
was waiting for me, you
fool?" she snapped back at
him.

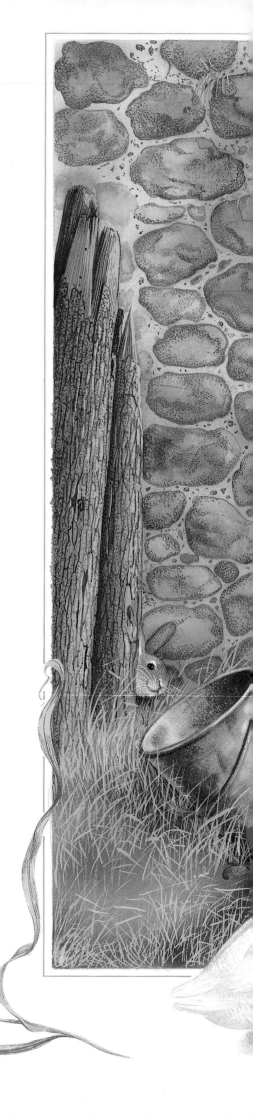

Constant was wild with temper and stamped his foot and called his dogs and all his men and off they went, with sticks and staves and hoes and rakes. Dogs barked, pigs squealed, and cats, ducks, geese and dust flew up in all directions.

The air was full with cries of "Over here!", "This way!", "That way!", "Over there!" and "Curse the rogue!", "Catch him!" and "Tally-ho!"

The fox leapt hedges,
ditches and dykes. Now
Chantecler was almost lost.
He hadn't got a lot of
brain, but what he had he
must use now. "Friend," he
croaked, "you hear those
dreadful things they are
shouting? Why not hurl
back an insult of your own?
Show them who is master
hereabouts. That'll make
them mad." And Reynard,
wise though he was, could
not resist, for he was
cunning, he was clever, but
he was also very pleased
with himself.

As he opened his mouth to taunt them, out flew the squawking, tattered cockerel up into the pear tree that stood near by, leaving Reynard aghast beneath him.

"Well now friend," crowed Chantecler, "what have you got to say to that?"

"Nothing!" snapped Reynard, who could hardly speak through fury, "but...but...oh, bother a mouth that opens when it should stay shut."

"Mmm," replied Chantecler, in deepest thought, "and may I say it? Bother an eye that shuts when it should stay open!"

So Chantecler had escaped.
He was the worse for wear
but wiser, and when he was
back in the farmyard he
boasted to all who would
listen, in a loud crowing
voice, all about his great
adventure and how he had
foiled the fox.

And as for Reynard? Well,
he was wiser too – but he
was still hungry!

The End